Inside a RAIN FOREST

Written by Gare Thompson

Steck Vaughn™

HOUGHTON MIFFLIN HARCOURT
Supplemental Publishers

www.SteckVaughn.com
800-531-5015

The trees are very tall. The flowers are colorful and beautiful. It is always rainy and hot. Many interesting animals live there. Where is this place? It is the rain forest. There are only a few places like this on Earth.

Rain Forest

Many animals make their home in the rain forest. Huge cats, such as tigers and jaguars, move quietly below the trees. Monkeys chatter and swing high up in the trees. Large sloths and lemurs hang from tree branches. Sloths spend most of their days in trees, sleeping upside-down.

Sloth

The sounds of many different birds fill the rain forest air. Macaw parrots and parakeets sing from the trees. Toucans gather fruit in their huge beaks. Birds called hoatzins climb through trees using the claws they have on each wing. Eagles watch from above for a meal.

Toucan

The rain forest also has animals that slither and crawl. It is hard to spot the congo and anaconda snakes hanging in trees or slithering across the forest floor. But it is quite easy to see the colorful tree frogs. Some are red with polka dots, and others are bright lime green.

Anaconda

Thousands of insects live in rain forests. Ants work at moving leaves and food from place to place. The sky gets dark as mosquitoes buzz through the air. Butterflies glide above the many flowers and plants.

Butterfly

Tall trees and plants form the layers in the rain forest. The trees make a roof over the forest. Their leaves make a canopy. Shade from the tall trees traps in heat and wetness. This helps plants grow all year around.

Canopy

Other plants that grow in the rain forest have beautiful green leaves and colorful flowers. The world's largest flower grows there. Many of the plants in the rain forest are used to make things, such as rubber. Some are even used to make medicines.

Rafflesia, World's Largest Flower

Rain forests are like no other place on Earth. But some are in danger of being destroyed. People have cut down many trees and taken plants and animals away. Rain forests need people to protect them. What are some ways you might help?